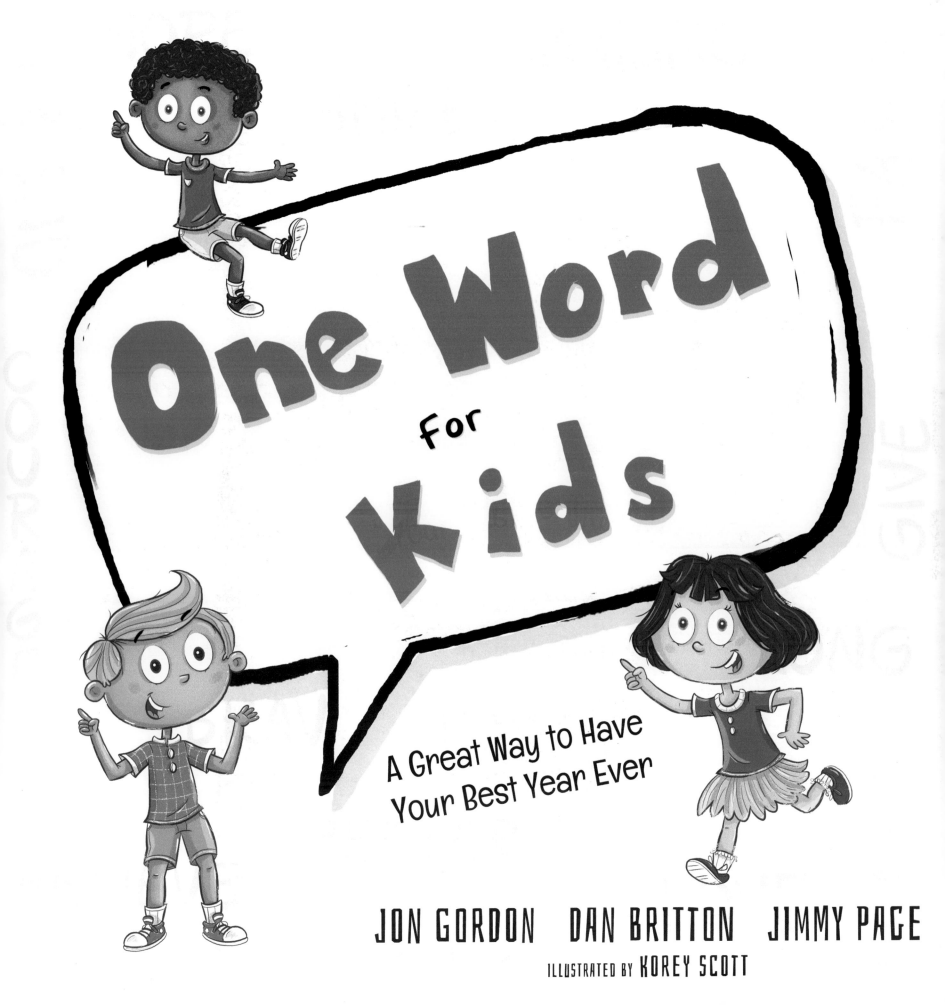

One Word for Kids

A Great Way to Have Your Best Year Ever

JON GORDON DAN BRITTON JIMMY PAGE

ILLUSTRATED BY KOREY SCOTT

For general information on our other products and services or for technical support, please contact our Customer Care Department within the United States at (800) 762-2974, outside the United States at (317) 572-3993 or fax (317) 572-4002.

Wiley publishes in a variety of print and electronic formats and by print-on-demand. Some material included with standard print versions of this book may not be included in e-books or in print-on-demand. If this book refers to media such as a CD or DVD that is not included in the version you purchased, you may download this material at http://booksupport.wiley.com. For more information about Wiley products, visit www.wiley.com.

ISBN 9781119430315 (Hardcover)
ISBN 9781119430889 (ePDF)
ISBN 9781119430896 (ePub)

Printed in the United States of America.

W328555_092419

Jimmy, Dan, and Jon dedicate this book to their children, respectively:

Jimmy, Jake, John, and Grace

Kallie, Abby, and Elijah

Jade and Cole

It was the first day of school and Stevie was falling asleep. He was tired, grumpy, and sad that summer was over.

But his ears perked up when his teacher, Mrs. B, said,
"I believe there is *one word* that will help you have your
best year ever. It will be so great you'll enjoy it even
more than summer vacation."

Stevie's friend Eli raised his hand and asked,
"What word is that?"

"The word will likely be different for everyone,"
Mrs. B said. "I have a special assignment for each
of you. It's to find your own *one word* for the year."

"So, how do we find it?" Stevie's classmate Jimmy asked.

"I will help you, but I want you to try to discover it on your own first," Mrs. B answered.

That night, while having dinner with his family, Stevie wouldn't talk or eat. When his mom asked what was wrong, he told her about the *one word* assignment. He was sad, because he had no idea how to find his *one word*.

"Maybe your *one word* is annoying!" his sister Kallie shouted.
"I think it should be negative!" his sister Jade yelled.

"C'mon, girls," Stevie's dad quickly responded. "Stevie, maybe you should think about some of the things you love to do or your favorite places to go. Maybe you'll find your *one word* there."

That night, Stevie went to bed and thought about all his favorite places and things he loves to do, hoping he'd find his *one word*.

Maybe my *one word* is "FUN."

Maybe my *one word* is "LOVE."

Maybe my *one word* is "KIND."

Maybe my *one word* is "SMILE."

Maybe my *one word* is "STRONG."

Maybe my *one word* is "BRAVE."

14

The next morning, Stevie woke up excited. He was still thinking about all the words he could choose.

When school started, Mrs. B said, "I have great news for all of you! Today, I'm going to give you the secret to finding your *one word*!"

"What's the first step?" Abby yelled.

"The first step is to look into your heart," Mrs. B said.
"Ask yourself, 'What *one word* will help me be my best?'"

"The second step is to look up," said Mrs. B.
"Look up and around and believe that there is *one word* meant for you. If you're open to it, it will come to you."

"What's the third step?" Cole asked.

"That comes after you know your *one word*," Mrs. B answered. "I'll tell you that step soon, but first, who's ready to discover their *one word*?"

All the students cheered!

On the bus ride home, Stevie thought about the first step.
He thought about words that would help him be his best.

As Stevie walked off the bus, he waved to his friend George and said goodbye to Miss Joy, the bus driver.

"Thank you, sugar! I love how positive you are today!" Miss Joy said.

24

That night, as Stevie walked his dog, Huxley, he thought about all the possible words. He looked up and remembered what Miss Joy said to him as he got off the bus. In that moment, his *one word* came to him. **POSITIVE!**

He remembered how grumpy he had been when summer was over. Mrs. B said his *one word* would help him have his best year ever. He now knew his *one word* was POSITIVE and he couldn't wait to tell everyone!

Stevie ran home and told his family.

POSITIVE

The next day, Stevie walked into school feeling good that he had discovered his *one word*.

"Alright class, today is the day! Tell me your words!" Mrs. B said.

"Mine is 'CARE'!" Dawn said.

"COURAGE!" Xavier said.

Ivelisse said, "My *one word* is 'BELIEVE'!"

"Mine is 'FAITH'!" Kathryn said.

"Class, I am so proud of each and every one of you!" Mrs. B said. "Here is the best part. The third and last step is to look out and live your *one word*."

On the bus ride home, Stevie was extra positive with Miss Joy!

At soccer practice, Stevie encouraged his teammates and even shared the *one word* idea with his coach. His coach loved the idea and shared it with the team.

Stevie lived his *one word* for the entire school year
and, on the last day of school, he realized that
Mrs. B was right. He had his best year ever, and it
was even better than summer vacation.

If *one word* can help Stevie, think about what *one word* can do for you.

My *one word* is

_____ .

OTHER BOOKS BY THE AUTHORS

One Word

One Word is a simple concept that delivers powerful life change! This quick read will inspire you to simplify your life and work by focusing on just one word for this year. *One Word* creates clarity, power, passion, and life change. When you find your word, live it, and share it, your life will become more rewarding and exciting than ever.

www.getoneword.com

Twitter: @GetOneWord

Facebook: Facebook.com/GetOneWord

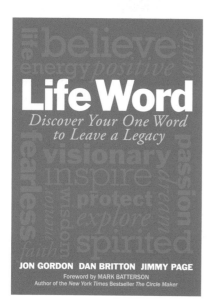

Life Word

Life Word reveals a simple, powerful tool to help you identify the word that will inspire you to live your best life while leaving your greatest legacy. In the process, you'll discover your *why*, which will help show you how to live with a renewed sense of power, purpose, and passion.

www.getoneword.com/lifeword

OTHER CHILDREN'S BOOKS BY JON GORDON

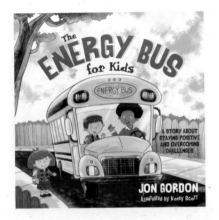

The Energy Bus for Kids

The illustrated children's adaptation of the bestselling book *The Energy Bus* tells the story of George, who, with the help of his school bus driver, Joy, learns that if he believes in himself, he'll find the strength to overcome any challenge. His journey teaches kids how to overcome negativity, bullies, and everyday challenges to be their best.

www.EnergyBusKids.com

The Hard Hat for Kids

The Hard Hat for Kids is an illustrated guide to teamwork. Adapted from the bestseller *The Hard Hat*, this uplifting story presents practical insights and life-changing lessons that are immediately applicable to everyday situations, giving kids—and adults—a new outlook on cooperation, friendship, and the selfless nature of true teamwork.

www.HardHatforKids.com

Thank You and Good Night

Thank You and Good Night is a beautifully illustrated book that shares the heart of gratitude. Jon Gordon takes a little boy and girl on a fun-filled journey from one perfect moonlit night to the next. During their adventurous days and nights, the children explore the people, places, and things they are thankful for.

BRING *ONE WORD* TO YOUR SCHOOLS

Jon, Dan, and Jimmy are passionate about investing in schools, educators, coaches, and kids. Over the past 20 years, they have worked with countless school districts that have utilized *One Word* throughout their schools and teams. *One Word* enhances morale, improve teacher performance and motivates students.

Programs include:

- *One Word* Workshops and Keynotes for Teachers and Administrators

- School Assemblies

- Readings in the Classroom with Illustrator Korey Scott

For more information contact the Jon Gordon Companies and ask about *One Word*:

Phone: (904) 285-6842

Email: info@jongordon.com

Web: www.getoneword.com

Twitter: @getoneword

Facebook: @getoneword

Instagram: @getoneword

COMPLEMENTARY RESOURCES

For free resources, visit: www.getoneword.com/kids

One Word Action Plan for Schools

These free action plans will help you through the 3-step process of Looking IN, Looking UP, and Looking OUT. The action plan for schools will help teachers and coaches implement *One Word* with their classroom and teams.

4-Day Reading Plan

Join over 1 million people who have downloaded the *One Word* You Version devotional and discover your *One Word*.

One Word Posters

Create your own *One Word* poster *and* share it in the classroom and around the school! Choose from 3 different designs.

One Word Podcast

This podcast features Jon, Jimmy, and Dan sharing how *One Word* was developed and how to maximize your *One Word*.

Discussion Guide for Groups and Teams

This discussion guide can be used with your company's leadership team, sports team, small group, family or just with another person. There are five sessions for you to utilize as you read through the book.

STRONG
BELIEVE
BETTER
SMILE
AMAZING
FAMILY
COURAGE
GIVE
FUN
FRIEND
THANKFUL
LOVE
BRAVE
HEART
HAPPY
KIND
HOPE